SUPERHERO JOE

WRITTEN BY JACQUELINE PREISS WEITZMAN
DRAWN BY RON BARRETT

A PAULA WISEMAN BOOK
Simon & Schuster Books for Young Readers
New York • London • Toronto • Sydney

FOR MY FAVORITE SUPERHEROES,
WILL AND ALEX
—J. P. W.

SIMON & SCHUSTER BOOKS FOR YOUNG READERS
AN IMPRINT OF SIMON & SCHUSTER CHILDREN'S PUBLISHING DIVISION
1230 AVENUE OF THE AMERICAS, NEW YORK, NEW YORK 10020
TEXT COPYRIGHT © 2011 BY JACQUELINE PREISS WEITZMAN
ILLUSTRATIONS COPYRIGHT © 2011 BY RONALD BARRETT
ALL RIGHTS RESERVED, INCLUDING THE RIGHT OF REPRODUCTION IN
WHOLE OR IN PART IN ANY FORM.
SIMON & SCHUSTER BOOKS FOR YOUNG READERS IS A
TRADEMARK OF SIMON & SCHUSTER, INC.
FOR INFORMATION ABOUT SPECIAL DISCOUNTS FOR BULK PURCHASES,
PLEASE CONTACT SIMON & SCHUSTER SPECIAL SALES AT 1-866-506-1949
OR BUSINESS@SIMONANDSCHUSTER.COM.
THE SIMON & SCHUSTER SPEAKERS BUREAU CAN BRING AUTHORS TO YOUR LIVE
EVENT. FOR MORE INFORMATION OR TO BOOK AN EVENT, CONTACT THE SIMON &
SCHUSTER SPEAKERS BUREAU AT 1-866-248-3049 OR VISIT OUR WEBSITE AT
WWW.SIMONSPEAKERS.COM.
BOOK DESIGN BY RON BARRETT
THE TEXT FOR THIS BOOK IS HAND LETTERED.
THE ILLUSTRATIONS FOR THIS BOOK ARE RENDERED IN INK AND COLORED
DIGITALLY.
MANUFACTURED IN CHINA
0611 SCP
2 4 6 8 10 9 7 5 3 1
LIBRARY OF CONGRESS CATALOGING-IN-PUBLICATION DATA
WEITZMAN, JACQUELINE PREISS.
SUPERHERO JOE / JACQUELINE PREISS WEITZMAN ;
ILLUSTRATED BY RON BARRETT. — 1ST ED.
P. CM.
"A PAULA WISEMAN BOOK."
SUMMARY: FIVE-YEAR-OLD JOEY USES HIS SUPERPOWERS TO HELP HIS PARENTS
OUT OF A STICKY SITUATION.
ISBN 978-1-4169-9157-1 (HARDCOVER)
[1. SUPERHEROES—FICTION. 2. IMAGINATION—FICTION. 3. FEAR—FICTION.]
I. BARRETT, RON, ILL. II. TITLE.
PZ7.W4481843SU 2011
[E]—DC22
2009034390
ISBN 978-1-4424-3504-9 (EBOOK)

SHE PLEADED WITH ME TO BRING HER THE STAFF OF POWER, WHICH WOULD HELP HER BANISH THE OOZE.

AND THERE PROBABLY AREN'T ANY MONSTERS IN MY CLOSET.